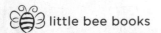 little bee books

An imprint of Bonnier Publishing USA
251 Park Avenue South, New York, NY 10010
Copyright © 2017 by Bonnier Publishing USA
All rights reserved, including the right of reproduction in whole or in part in any form. LITTLE BEE BOOKS is a trademark of Bonnier Publishing USA, and associated colophon is a trademark of Bonnier Publishing USA.
Library of Congress Cataloging-in-Publication Data is available upon request.

Printed in the United States of America LB 0617
ISBN 978-1-4998-0409-6 (hc)
First Edition 10 9 8 7 6 5 4 3 2 1
ISBN 978-1-4998-0371-6 (pb)
First Edition 10 9 8 7 6 5 4 3 2 1
littlebeebooks.com
bonnierpublishingusa.com

ELLA AND OWEN

THE EVIL PUMPKIN PIE FIGHT

by
Jaden Kent

little bee books

illustrated by
Iryna Bodnaruk

TABLE OF CONTENTS

1: A HEAD FOR TROUBLE 1

2: ALL HAIL THE PUMPKIN KING! 13

3: WHAT A TANGLED WEB 23

4: WARTS UP? 37

5: WARTY WART HAG FACE 47

6: PUMPKIN PIE PANDEMONIUM 57

7: STICKY BUSINESS 71

8: DING DONG, THE WITCH IS WED 83

9: THE PARTY'S OVER 89

① A HEAD FOR TROUBLE

"Give us me wishes!" Dumberdoor the troll said.

"We found the pink platypus that plays the ukulele upside down!" Dumbdalf, the other troll, said. "Now you owe us wishes."

The two trolls raced out from the forest toward Ella and Owen.

The dragon twins were shocked.

"How did they find a pink platypus?" Owen asked his sister.

"I don't even want to know about the ukulele," she replied.

"So, where's me wishes?" Dumberdoor demanded.

"Okay, okay. I have your first wish," Owen said. The trolls rubbed their hairy, wart-covered hands together with excitement.

"Your first wish is that you wish you could watch me and Ella run away!" Owen and Ella turned and ran away.

"Me not want that wish!" Dumberdoor said. "Me wish for dragon stew!"

"Me, too, wish for stew dragon!" Dumbdalf added. "Grant me wish!"

The trolls watched as the two dragons ran into the forest and disappeared into the shadows.

"I think we lost them," Ella said.

"I hope so," Owen puffed. "My claws are aching from all that running and my wings are too tired to flutter."

Owen looked around. "Wait a minute! We're back in Terror Swamp again! I didn't want that either!"

"Don't worry. I think home is this way," Ella said, pointing through the trees, ". . . or maybe it's that way."

"Good," Owen replied. "You go that way. I'm going the other way." Owen ran away but crashed into a tree. A branch broke off and fell on his head. "It's a Swamp Tree Goblin! It's got me!" Owen's scaly body wobbled and he tripped over a tree stump. He crashed into Ella.

"Watch where you're going!" she cried.

Ella and Owen splashed down into the inky black doom of Terror Swamp.

Ella shivered, shaking the water from her scales. "Don't be such a scaredy-dragon," she said. "There's hardly any water here."

Owen stood up and picked the mud off of his claws. "Great. So we're lost again."

"Maybe not," she replied. Ella pointed toward something moving on the other side of some trees. There was a flickering light in the distance. "Let's check that out," she said.

"Oh, let's not," Owen replied. "Every time we go check out something, we get captured and something tries to eat us."

"It could be a way out of Terror Swamp," she said.

"Really?!" Owen said. "There's no way I'm going to investigate the *only* light glowing in the middle of a place called Terror Swamp!" Owen folded his scaly arms. He wasn't budging.

"Well, I'm going to go see what it is. You can stay here. On your own. In the dark." Ella's dragon wings fluttered and she flew off toward the light.

Owen looked around as it grew darker. Leaves rustled and swirled in the night air.

A Grizzly Owl hooted.

A Swamp Bat swooped low, passing by Owen's snout.

On second thought, being left all alone while someone else goes to check out the only light glowing in the middle of a place called Terror Swamp is even worse than going to check out the only light glowing in the middle of a place called Terror Swamp! Owen thought.

Owen flew off after his sister. "Okay, Ella! Wait up! Let's see what's making that light!"

Together, the two dragons pushed through the forest. They came to a clearing in front of a broken-down wooden swamp shack. A jack-o'-lantern with an angry face carved into it sat on the porch. Light flickered from the candle inside of it.

"That's one creepy jack-o'-lantern!" Ella said.

"Okay, we've seen what the light is. Let's leave," Owen said. "This place looks haunted."

"You can't ever go," the jack-o'-lantern suddenly said to them. "Ever-never!"

"Who-who are you?" Ella stuttered.

"I am . . . the Pumpkin King!" he said. "Vines up!"

"AHHHHHHHH!" Ella and Owen screamed.

Vines stretched out from beneath the porch and wrapped around Ella and Owen.

"I told you something like this would happen!" Owen yelled.

2
ALL HAIL THE PUMPKIN KING!

"Just what are you the king of?" Ella asked. The Pumpkin King's head sat on the wooden floor inside the swamp shack. The dragon siblings sat on the floor, wrapped tightly in leafy green vines.

"Right now, I'm the king of, well . . . just this shack," the Pumpkin King replied. "But I have very big plans for next year! Soon

I'll be king of those rocks over there and maybe those bushes right outside the front door."

"It's good to have dreams," Owen said. "Can you let us go now?"

"Never!" the Pumpkin King said. "You're working for the witch! She already stole my body, and now you're here to steal my royal crown!"

Ella and Owen saw the king's "crown" resting on a broken chair. The crown was made of twigs and pinecones. A beetle crawled lazily across it.

"Looks . . . um . . . fantastic," Ella said. Owen snorted, and Ella elbowed him to keep him from laughing.

"You try making a crown without any arms and see how well you do!" the Pumpkin King huffed.

"We don't work for anyone!" Ella said.

"And we don't know any witches either," said Owen.

"We're just lost," Ella explained.

"We want out of Terror Swamp and we want to go home!" Owen explained.

"If you're not spies, maybe we can make a deal," the Pumpkin King said.

"What kind of deal?" asked Ella.

"A royal deal! I'll give you a map that will take you out of Terror Swamp," the Pumpkin King said.

TERRIBLE WITCH LIVES HERE

CREEPY GRAVEYARD

WAY OUT

TERROR SWAMP

"That's great!" Owen said.

"And in return, you have to go GET MY BODY BACK FROM THAT WITCH!"

"Why can't you just go get your body back yourself?" Ella asked.

"I've been growing a pumpkin army to attack that witch and steal back my body, but it's taking way too long," the Pumpkin King explained. "Did you know that pumpkins take months to grow? And pumpkin kings are terrible farmers. Also, I've got this itch that's killing me. And don't even ask me about how hard it is to make pies without a body!"

"Uh, pies?" Owen asked.

"Yes! Pies!" the Pumpkin King snapped, tilting his head to motion to the stacks and stacks of pies in the corner of his shack.

"That's a LOT of pies," Ella gasped.

"Eleventy-raccoon at last count!" the Pumpkin King proudly announced.

"Uh, 'eleventy-raccoon' isn't a number," Ella said.

"Whattya expect?! My head's *hollow*, okay?!" the Pumpkin King griped. "Also, math wasn't required at Pumpkin King School."

"Okay, we'll help you," Ella agreed.

"Wait! We'll do *what*?" Owen exclaimed.

"In exchange for the map," Ella added.

19

"Can you throw in something to eat, too? A little fire thorn stew?" Owen suggested. "Fish bone casserole? Screamer Beetle nachos with extra screams?"

"All I have are pumpkin seeds," the Pumpkin King replied.

"We'll still do it," Ella said. She grabbed a handful of seeds that were scattered around the shack and popped them into her mouth. Then she grabbed another handful for later.

"So this witch . . ." Owen began. "I'll bet she lives on the other side of a creepy graveyard?"

"No," the Pumpkin King corrected.

"Whew! That's a relief!" Owen replied.

"She lives in the *middle* of a creepy graveyard," the Pumpkin King finished.

"Great," Owen said with a groan.

3

WHAT A TANGLED WEB

"It's quiet," Owen whispered. "Too quiet."

"Shhhhh!" Ella whispered back. "It's not quiet if you keep talking."

Ella and Owen tiptoed through the dark graveyard. Headstones stuck out from the mossy ground. Leafy vines

hung from trees and wrapped around their trunks. Owls hooted. Bats flew overhead. Wind rattled the iron gates of the cemetery. A thick fog covered the ground.

"Watch your step, Ella," Owen said. "I can't see my claws in the fog and—oof!" Owen tripped over a headstone and fell to the ground. *"OUCH!"*

"Shhhh!"

"No one can hear us in a graveyard," Owen said.

"I know. I just hate graveyards," Ella whispered. "They remind me of cemeteries."

"Graveyards and cemeteries are the same thing," Owen said.

"That explains it, then," Ella whispered back.

"Don't tell me you're suddenly afraid," Owen said. "One of us has to be a brave dragon."

"I'm not afraid of the dark," she replied. "I'm not afraid of bats, rats, vampires, or even witches." She paused and took a deep breath. "But I am afraid of zombies."

"Zombies? They're already dead. You can't be afraid of dead things."

"They eat dragon brains," Ella said. "And I'd prefer my brain to stay in my head."

"Okay then, since you want out of here faster, you go first," Owen said.

"Well, since you're not scared of zombies, *you* go first," Ella said, nudging Owen forward.

"Since you're more scared than I am, you go first more," Owen said. He pushed Ella to take the lead.

"Who dares disturb my slumber?" A ghostly specter rose up from the ground.

"Okay! Now I'm scared!" Owen gasped.

"I'm scared more!" Ella said.

"Not as much as I am!" Owen said.

"Like ten bajillion times more than you!" Ella replied.

"Um, excuse me," the ghost said. "Remember me? Angry ghost? In the cemetery?"

"Be with you in a sec, Mr. Ghost," Owen said then turned back to Ella. "Well, *I'm* waaaay more scared than if I woke up and found a thousand headless Screamer Scorpions crawling under my pillow!"

"Uh, guys?" the ghost interrupted.

They both ignored the ghost and continued to argue over who was more scared.

"And *I'm* even more scared than if I woke up and found out that I looked like *you*!" Ella said to Owen.

"**WOOOOO-HOOOOOOO!**" the ghost howled. Ella's and Owen's wings shivered. The ghostly voice had stopped Ella and Owen from arguing. They flew backward in a panic . . . and landed in a huge spiderweb.

"Okay, now I'm really scared," Owen said. He tried to pull himself out of the web. "And we're stuck, too."

"I'd love to help," the ghost said, "but I really don't like spiders." He sunk back into the ground and disappeared.

"Don't move," Owen said to Ella.

"Why?" she asked.

"Unless I'm mistaken, this is the web of a giant twelve-fanged Vampire Tree Spider," he said. "I've seen pictures of them in a book called *Spiders That Can Eat a Dragon*. Oh no! It's seen us!"

The giant twelve-fanged Vampire Tree Spider slid out from a web tunnel at the top of the tree. It slowly and hungrily creeped toward Ella and Owen.

"Did you ever notice that a lot of things want to eat us lately?" Ella asked. She tugged on the web and kicked as hard as she could. She was stuck, too.

"Of course they do," Owen replied. "*I'm* very tasty."

The spider moved closer. Its eight hairy legs skated across the web.

"Tasty! That's it! Ella, do you still have those seeds from the Pumpkin King?"

"Food? You're thinking about food when we're about to *be* food?!" Ella yelled.

"Let's give the spider something that isn't dragon meat!" Owen cried.

The spider crept right up to the trapped dragons. Drool dripped from its hungry mouth. It was close enough for Owen to count ten of its twelve fangs.

The spider jumped at Ella, eager for a yummy dragon snack. Ella ducked and threw her extra pumpkin seeds into the spider's mouth.

The spider happily gobbled them down and burped. No longer hungry, it crawled to the edge of its web and lay down to sleep. It would not be eating two dragons . . . yet.

"Nice job, Ella!" Owen yelled. He finally managed to hook one of his thumb claws into the web and cut them free.

The two dragons plopped to the ground and took off.

WARTS UP?

"Okay, now *that* looks spooky," Owen said. "I told you we shouldn't have come here."

The witch's home sat in the middle of the cemetery, just like the Pumpkin King had said. The cottage was quiet and still. Moss covered much of the roof, and many of the windows were dark. But a light in one window suggested someone was inside.

"How are we supposed to sneak in and get the Pumpkin King's body back from the witch?" Owen asked.

"I have an idea," Ella said. She grabbed some mud and slapped it onto Owen's face, covering him with moss and swamp muck.

"Ow, I'm going to get scale warts!" Owen complained.

"Quiet, please," Ella said. "I'm making you into something witches love: a zombie."

The mud covered Owen's entire face. "Yuck!" he said. Ella stuck a couple of twigs and leaves onto Owen's muddy face. "But you're scared of zombies."

39

"I am. But I've heard that witches love zombies," she said. Then she slapped mud onto her own face and spread it all around, covering her long snout.

"Now we just walk and talk like two mindless zombies," Ella explained. "Then we can knock on the witch's door and she'll let us in." She smiled. "And that's when we take back the Pumpkin King's body."

Ella and Owen stumbled in the direction of the witch's house. Owen held one leg stiff and dragged it along the ground. Ella stretched out her arms in front of her body.

"Braaaaains," Ella groaned. "Must . . . have . . . braaaains!"

"Chocolate caaaaake," Owen groaned. Ella glared at him. "What?! I don't wanna eat brains! They're gross!"

They lumbered up to the front door of the cottage. Ella banged on the door with her foot.

The door opened slightly. The witch peered out from behind it.

"Braaaaains," Ella groaned.

"Oh, zombies! I haven't had zombie guests for weeks!" the witch said. "What can I do for you delightful walking undead?"

"Braaaaains," Ella groaned again.

The witch nodded and turned to Owen, waiting for his answer.

"Ummmm . . . soup?" Owen groaned.

"What kind of zombie eats *soup*?" the witch asked.

"Don't mind him," Ella groaned. "He stopped making sense after I ate his . . . braaaaains."

The witch opened the door all the way. Ella and Owen stumbled inside. "Where are you zombies from anyway?"

"Zombie . . . ville?" Owen replied, not quite sure where zombies would come from.

"Zombieville? I've never heard of Zombieville," the witch replied.

"It's across the Zombie Bridge from Zombieburg," Ella added. "It's a very small village."

"Let's have lunch," the witch said. "I'm all out of brains and soup, but I do have a nice stew in my cauldron." She dipped a ladle into the pot and pulled out an oddly shaped object.

"AAAAAAAH! BRAINS!" Owen screamed and jumped into Ella's arms.

"It's not a brain! It's a *turnip*!" Ella said.

"AAAAAAAAH! TURNIPS!" Owen screamed. He jumped from Ella's grasp and into the witch's arms.

The witch fell over backward from his weight. Owen landed on top of her. **"OOF,"** she oofed.

"You're *not* really zombies!" the witch said.

"**A**w, dragon scales! How'd you know that we weren't zombies?" Ella asked, shocked. "Did you cast some powerful magic spell?"

"Didn't need to. Even the worst zombie knows the difference between a turnip and a brain. And the last time I checked, zombies don't have *tails*." The witch pointed to Ella's and Owen's tails sticking out from under their disguises.

"Oops," Ella said. Her green cheeks turned red with embarrassment. "I'm Ella and this is my brother, Owen."

"My name is Rainbow Sparkles," the witch said. "Why did you come to my cottage?"

"I thought witches were named stuff like Warty Wart Hag Face and Hairy Wart Hag Face and Warty Hairy Warty Wart . . . Hag Face," Owen said.

"You read too many books, kid," Rainbow Sparkles replied. "Now tell me why you're here or I'll turn you into puppies!"

"NOOOOOOO! Not that! Wait . . . *puppies*?" Owen said.

"Yeah. *All* the other witches turn people into toads and newts. BOR-ING! It is *so* hard to find a witch with any imagination!" Rainbow Sparkles complained, then proudly added, "I'm the only one doing cute puppies."

"Tell her why we're here," Owen whispered to Ella.

"And get turned into a puppy? No way!" Ella whispered back.

"Okay, I'll do it," Owen said. "But just think about how mad Mom and Dad will be when they find out you let some witch named Raincloud Popsicle or whatever turn me into a little dog."

"Dragon drool! I'd rather be a puppy!" Ella said and faced Rainbow Sparkles. "The Pumpkin King sent us here to get his body back. He said you, um, kinda . . . uh . . . sorta . . . stole it?"

Ella closed her eyes, folded her wings into her back, and got ready to be turned into a puppy.

"Don't worry, Sis. I promise to take you for a walk every day once you're a puppy," Owen whispered to Ella.

"Or probably every *other* day."

"That's a lie!" Rainbow Sparkles huffed. "I never stole anybody . . . or any *body*! The Pumpkin King's body came to live with me because its pumpkin head was grumpy and mean! The pumpkin head was always forcing his body to make pies. Pies, pies, and pies! Nothing but pies!"

"What's wrong with pies?" Ella asked, slowly opening her eyes.

"Nothing. But it'd be nice if he was allowed to bake a cake now and then! You know, just to mix things up," Rainbow Sparkles said.

"I have a question," Owen said.

"Yes?" Rainbow Sparkles replied.

"Are you gonna turn my sister into a puppy or what?" Owen asked. "'Cause I wanna name her Ruff-Ruff Doggy-Doggy Bark Face!"

Before Rainbow Sparkles could reply, the Pumpkin King's headless body, which was stuffed with straw like a scarecrow, stumbled into the room. Without its pumpkin head, the body couldn't see where it was walking and it bonked into the table, then a wall, then it walked into a closet before finding its way over to Rainbow Sparkles.

"The Pumpkin King's body wants to live with me because . . ." Rainbow Sparkles giggled and hugged the headless straw body. "We're in love!"

"You know what, Owen? This just got *really* weird," Ella said.

"**W**e've got good news and bad news, o' King," Ella said to the Pumpkin King after they returned to his shack. Her tail nervously wagged behind her. "The bad news is . . . your body's not coming back. But the good news is . . . you're invited to a wedding!"

The Pumpkin King's orange head turned red with anger! "NOT COMING BACK?!" he shouted. Pumpkin seeds shot from his mouth. "Grab all the pumpkin pies you can carry and follow me!"

The Pumpkin King hopped out to his garden and commanded, "Pumpkin army! Time to battle the witch!"

"But we're not fully grown yet, your royal orangeness," one of the softball-sized pumpkins said in a squeaky voice. "But we are cuuuuuute."

"Um, like, maybe if you could come back in a month or so, we'd be, like, totally big?" a second pumpkin squeaked.

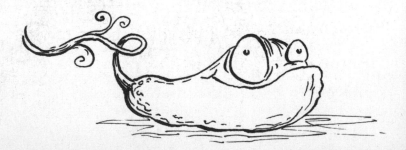

"I can't wait a month! If you're big enough to carry a pie, you're big enough to fight a witch!" the Pumpkin King responded as he bounced away from the swamp shack.

"Can't argue with that logic," Owen said to Ella.

Dozens of small pumpkins broke from their vines. Some were round and some were oblong. Some had lumps while others had bumps. They hopped along after the Pumpkin King like a mess of orange bouncing balls.

Ella and Owen fluttered along after the pumpkins, doing their best to carry the teetering towers of pumpkin pies they held in their clawed hands.

"Why are we helping him?" Owen asked. "He's kinda nuts."

"He's not kinda nuts. He's *completely* nuts," Ella replied. "But we've gotta get the Pumpkin King's map so we can get out of Terror Swamp. Just play along until we think of a plan."

Once they reached Rainbow Sparkles's cottage, the Pumpkin King ordered Owen and Ella to place a pie atop each of his pumpkin soldiers' heads.

"Are you gonna invite the witch to a picnic?" Owen asked.

"Yes. A picnic of doooooooom!" The Pumpkin King laughed.

"Maybe it'd be better if you just made her a sandwich?" Ella said.

"I'm in charge of the picnic—I mean battle—not you!" the Pumpkin King answered. "Launch the sandwiches—I mean pies—my pumpkin army!"

The pumpkins hopped off the ground
and launched the pumpkin pies from their
heads.

The pies hit Rainbow Sparkles's cottage
and splattered ooey, gooey pumpkin pie
filling everywhere, covering the entire
building.

"I'll get you for that, you grumpy ol' pumpkin head!" Rainbow Sparkles shouted as she ran from her cottage with the Pumpkin King's body beside her. She waved her wand and conjured up her own swarm of floating apple pies, which she then sent flying toward the Pumpkin King and his army.

SPLAT!

SPLAT!

Ella dove to her left to avoid being hit, but Owen wasn't fast enough and an apple pie hit him square in the snout.

SPLAT!

"This is the tastiest battle I've ever seen!" he said merrily, licking the pie from his face. "I hope someone starts throwing some creamy worm pies, too!"

Each side threw pie after pie at the other as chaos broke out. Rainbow Sparkles conjured up more pies out of thin air and threw them at the pumpkin army. Even the Pumpkin King's body was throwing pies but, as it didn't have eyes, only managed to throw them into some bushes.

"I know how we can stop this pie fight!" Ella said, dodging an apple pie.

"With an army of annoyed bananas?" Owen said.

"No! With a spider!" Ella replied and grabbed two pies. "Follow me!"

"Snails and tails! I'd rather try our luck with a whole mess of annoyed bananas." Owen sighed but followed his sister anyway.

"**L**ast chance to go find some annoyed bananas," Owen said as they ran back to the spiderweb that had held them earlier. "Or how about a grumpy papaya?"

"Nope. We stick with the plan," Ella replied.

"Is part of the plan getting eaten by a giant spider?" a nervous Owen asked.

"Of course not," Ella said.

"Then we better start flying!" Owen shouted.

"HISSSS!" the Vampire Tree Spider hissed as it spied the approaching dragons.

The huge spider jumped up and tried to pluck Owen and Ella out of the air and into its slobbery mandibles.

"Dragon wings, don't fail me now!" Owen said and quickly zoomed away.

Ella followed him, crushing up the pies in her hands and leaving a trail of pie crumbs behind her.

The spider happily gobbled up the bits of pie as it chased the two dragons.

Ella and Owen flapped their wings as quickly as they could and barely stayed ahead of the scampering spider just below them.

When they got back to Rainbow
Sparkles's cottage, both sides were still
throwing pies at each other, but now
Rainbow Sparkles was conjuring up
doughnuts as well. The Pumpkin King's
pumpkin army was covered in pie filling,
frosting, and doughnut sprinkles.

"This battle is worse than getting ice beetles stuck in your scales!" Ella said.

"I know! And it's a total waste of dessert, too!" Owen added gloomily.

But the <u>appearance</u> of the giant spider put an instant end to the battle. The spider spun a huge web, trapping Ella, Owen, the Pumpkin King, the pumpkin army, Rainbow Sparkles, and the Pumpkin King's body within it like flies.

"Hey! One of your crazy plans worked again, Sis!" Owen said. "But now how're we gonna stop the giant spider from eating us?"

"I kinda, sorta, didn't think about that part," Ella confessed.

The spider crept closer to Ella and Owen. Spider drool dripped onto Ella's wings.

"Wing warts! I hate spider drool!" Ella said.

"You'd better hope spiders like chocolate doughnuts or we're gonna be dragon-shaped spider snacks!" Owen flapped his wings as hard as he could and, despite being stuck in the web, managed to create a small breeze that blew a pile of doughnuts toward the spider. The spider sniffed them once, twice, then happily gobbled them up.

But the Pumpkin King was even angrier than before. "Get me out of this web!" he shouted.

"Don't worry. I saved a jelly-filled one for you," Owen assured him.

"I don't want a doughnut!" the Pumpkin King snarled, spitting pumpkin seeds from his mouth. "I. Want. My. BODY!"

"Your body wants to stay with Rainbow Sparkles," Ella explained.

"That's impossible!" the Pumpkin King huffed. "That witch cast a spell on my body. That's the only way it would want to stay with her."

"I did no such thing!" Rainbow Sparkles protested.

Despite the webbing that held them like glue, Rainbow Sparkles and the Pumpkin King's body managed to reach out and hug each other.

"We're in love!" Rainbow Sparkles giggled.

"Okay. This just got *really* weird," the Pumpkin King said.

Even a grouchy old thing like the Pumpkin King knew no pumpkin army could ever defeat the power of love, so he agreed that his body could marry Rainbow Sparkles. Luckily the spider liked chocolate doughnuts more than dragons, pumpkins, and witches, so it freed everyone from its web . . . as long as they kept feeding it doughnuts.

All the ghouls, banshees, ghosts, and goblins in Terror Swamp were invited to the wedding of Rainbow Sparkles and the Pumpkin King's body. Some zombies even lumbered over all the way from Zombie Town to join in the festivities.

Ella and Owen sat in the front row next to the now-less-grumpy-but-still-a-little-grumpy Pumpkin King, who wore a fancy top hat. The pumpkin army, dressed in matching tuxedoes, sang songs as Rainbow Sparkles, dressed in a wedding gown made of cobwebs, walked down the aisle with dead, black flowers hanging from a broomstick.

"Braaaaains . . ." a zombie in a ripped and dirty dress sitting next to Owen said.

"Sorry. Dinner's not until after the ceremony," Owen replied.

The ghostly specter from the graveyard floated over to the front of the gathering. "Dearly beloved . . . and dearly deceased, cursed, headless, haunted, and undead," he groaned loudly. "We are gathered here today to celebrate the wedding of Rainbow Sparkles the witch and the Pumpkin King's body, who wishes to be called Headless Joe."

"Bwaaaaaaaa!" the Pumpkin King blubbered. "I always cry at weddings. Especially when it's my body getting married."

Ella gently wiped away the Pumpkin King's tears. "We don't want you getting all moldy before they cut the wedding cake," she said.

Rainbow Sparkles and Headless Joe exchanged their rings, although Headless Joe, being unable to see because he had no head, stuck Rainbow Sparkles's ring on the end of her pointed nose.

"I now pronounce you witch and headless-body-stuffed-with-straw!" the ghostly specter announced with a groan.

Rainbow Sparkles and Headless Joe walked back down the aisle as their guests threw handfuls of beetles at them.

"This is easily the strangest wedding I've ever been to," Ella whispered to her brother.

"I know!" Owen agreed. "I can't wait to see how they celebrate birthdays!"

The wedding was over and the guests had all floated or lumbered home . . . or crawled back into the nearest grave.

"I can't thank you enough!" Rainbow Sparkles said to Ella and Owen. "None of this would've happened without your help."

"You know, if a kooky witch and a dude named Headless Joe can't find love in the nightmarish Terror Swamp, what hope do the rest of us have?" Owen said.

"You dragons kept your part of our deal," the Pumpkin King said. "It's not your fault my body wants someone else." He handed Owen a map that would lead them out of Terror Swamp.

"Thanks, Pumpkin King!" Owen replied.

"So, no more pie fights for you?" Ella asked.

"No. I never knew my pumpkin army was so talented until I heard them sing at the ceremony," the Pumpkin King explained. "So we're starting a singing group!"

"LAAAAAAAAAA!" the former pumpkin army sang in unison.

"We call ourselves the Smashing Pumpkins Pie," the Pumpkin King said proudly.

"Before we go, Owen and I want to give you guys some gifts, too," Ella said.

Ella put her fingers to her mouth, gave a loud whistle, and the giant Vampire Tree Spider drifted down from overhead, still eating chocolate doughnuts.

"We had the spider make you a new body!" Owen said to the Pumpkin King.

The spider held out a fancy new body woven from spider silk. Ella gently lifted the Pumpkin King and placed him atop the silky body.

"Thank you! It is so nice to have hands again!" The Pumpkin King scratched an itchy spot on the back of his lumpy head.

Owen handed Rainbow Sparkles a book. "And here's something for you and Headless Joe."

"A cake cookbook! I love it!" Rainbow Sparkles said. "Dear! Look what Ella and Owen got us!"

Rainbow Sparkles showed the cookbook to Headless Joe . . . who promptly walked into a tree.

"I'll just show it to him later," Rainbow Sparkles said.

With everyone happy, Owen and Ella said their final goodbyes and set off toward home. But little did they know that the two trolls, Dumberdoor and Dumbdalf, had not given up on their search for Ella and Owen and were in fact hiding behind some trees just down the trail from where the dragons were.

"Get the stew pot ready! Here come them two now!" Dumberdoor said.

"Us is gonna have a yummy dragon dinner tonight!" Dumbdalf replied as Ella and Owen made their way ever closer to the two hidden trolls. . . .

Read on for a sneak peek from the
fifth book in the Ella and Owen series!

ELLA AND OWEN

BOOK 5

THE GREAT TROLL QUEST

by Jaden Kent

illustrated by Iryna Bodnaruk

Ella and Owen ran through the forest. Their clawed feet crackled on the dried leaves scattered on the ground.

The Pumpkin King had kept his word. In return for Ella's and Owen's help in ending his feud with the witch Rainbow Sparkles, the Pumpkin King gave them a map that would take them out of Terror Swamp and back home to Dragon Patch.

"I think I should look at the map because I read a lot more than you do," Owen explained and grabbed the map from his sister with his claws.

"But I'm holding it!" Ella said. She pulled it away from Owen.

RiP! The map tore in half.

"Now you've done it," Ella accused.

"I should be the one to put it back together," Owen said. "I'm good at puzzles."

"No, I should put it back together because you ripped it apart," Ella replied. She grabbed for the two halves of the map with her claws.

RiP!

The halves of the map tore in half. The map was now in four pieces.

Ella and Owen looked at the pieces. "This is all YOUR fault!" they said to each other.

"I think we should stop," Owen suggested. "My dragon math powers aren't strong enough to figure out what half of a half of a half of a map is if we tear it again. I'll put it back together." Owen reached for a sticky, slicky slug from the leaf of a nearby prickly stickly tree.

"Gross! Tell me you're not going

to eat that," Ella said.

"Not this time. Watch." Owen slid the slug along the edges of the map fragments. Its pasty slime was sticky like glue and Owen got to work connecting the map pieces together.

"This piece goes here and that one goes there and—argh! Oops," Owen said. "I think I glued a piece of the map to myself."

A square of the map was stuck to Owen's scaly belly. Ella grabbed it and pulled.

"OWWW!" Owen yelped.

"It's really stuck! That slug slime is really sticky!"

Ella pulled harder. Owen stumbled forward into his sister and their bellies smacked together and got stuck.

Together, they rolled down the path, crashed into a tree stump, and flew into the air.

Map pieces scattered as the dragons plopped to the ground and split apart, landing right at the feet of Dumbdalf the troll.

"Us been looking all over the forest for you two!" Dumbdalf snarled.

Ella and Owen screamed.

Ella grabbed a piece of the map. "Here! We'll go this way!" she said, panicked.

Owen and Ella quickly turned away from Dumbdalf, but ran into his brother, Dumberdoor, coming down the path.

Owen grabbed another map piece off the ground. "This way!" Owen yelped.

The two dragons flew in the other direction away from Dumberdoor, but the troll had blocked that escape, too.

"Reading maps hurts my head." Owen handed the map pieces to his sister. "You read it now."